# Bob Met Ben

Practising CVC words with short
vowel sounds plus "and"

First published in 2007 by
Franklin Watts
338 Euston Road
London
NW1 3BH

Franklin Watts Australia
Hachette Children's Books
Level 17/207 Kent Street
Sydney
NSW 2000

A CIP catalogue record for this book is available
from the British Library.

ISBN: 978 0 7496 7120 4 (hbk)
ISBN: 978 0 7496 7307 9 (pbk)

**Series Editor:** Jackie Hamley
**Series Advisors:** Dr Barrie Wade, Dr Hilary Minns
**Series Designer:** Peter Scoulding


Printed in China

Franklin Watts is a division of
Hachette Children's Books.

# Bob Met Ben

by
Anne Adeney

Illustrated by
Anni Axworthy

W

FRANKLIN WATTS
LONDON·SYDNEY

**Anne Adeney**
"My children had lots of play dates like these. They always found it much more fun to play with other people's toys!"

**Anni Axworthy**
"The ideas for the drawings in this book were very easy. I just had to look at the floor of my house!"

# Bob met Ben.

# Bob had a van.

# Bob had ten.

9

# Bob had a dog.

# Ben had ten.

# Ben had a jet.

# Bob had ten.

# Bob had a cab.

# Ben had ten.

16

17

# Ben had a lot.

19

Bob had a lot.

# Bob and Ben had fun!

# Notes for parents and teachers

READING CORNER PHONICS has been structured to provide maximum support for children learning to read through synthetic phonics. The stories are designed for independent reading but may also be used by adults for sharing with young children.

The teaching of early reading through synthetic phonics focuses on the 44 sounds in the English language, and how these sounds correspond to their written form in the 26 letters of the alphabet. Carefully controlled vocabulary makes these books accessible for children at different stages of phonics teaching, progressing from simple CVC (consonant-vowel-consonant) words such as "top" (t-o-p) to trisyllabic words such as "messenger" (mess-en-ger). READING CORNER PHONICS allows children to read words in context, and also provides visual clues and repetition to further support their reading. These books will help develop the all important confidence in the new reader, and encourage a love of reading that will last a lifetime!

If you are reading this book with a child, here are a few tips:

**1.** Talk about the story before you start reading. Look at the cover and the title. What might the story be about? Why might the child like it?

**2.** Encourage the child to reread the story, and to retell the story in their own words, using the illustrations to remind them what has happened.

**3.** Discuss the story and see if the child can relate it to their own experience, or perhaps compare it to another story they know.

**4.** Give praise! Small mistakes need not always be corrected. If a child is stuck on a word, ask them to try and sound it out and then blend it together again, or model this yourself. For example "wish" w-i-sh "wish".

READING CORNER PHONICS covers two grades of synthetic phonics teaching, with three levels at each grade. Each level has a certain number of words per story, indicated by the number of bars on the spine of the book:

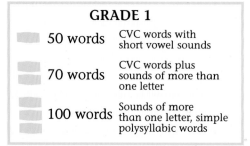

### GRADE 1

| | | |
|---|---|---|
| | 50 words | CVC words with short vowel sounds |
| | 70 words | CVC words plus sounds of more than one letter |
| | 100 words | Sounds of more than one letter, simple polysyllabic words |

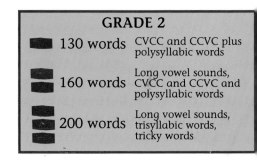

### GRADE 2

| | | |
|---|---|---|
| | 130 words | CVCC and CCVC plus polysyllabic words |
| | 160 words | Long vowel sounds, CVCC and CCVC and polysyllabic words |
| | 200 words | Long vowel sounds, trisyllabic words, tricky words |